Liv

The Owls of Blossom Wood

Emrie

Text copyright © 2015 by Catherine Coe
Illustrations copyright © 2015 by Renée Kurilla

All rights reserved. Published by Scholastic Inc., *Publishers since 1920.* SCHOLASTIC and associated logos are trademarks and/or registered trademarks of Scholastic Inc.

First published in the United Kingdom in 2015 by Scholastic Children's UK.

The publisher does not have any control over and does not assume any responsibility for author or third-party websites or their content.

ISBN 978-0-545-92891-5

10 9 8 7 6 5 4 3 2 1   16 17 18 19 20

Printed in the U.S.A.   40
This edition first printing 2016

The Owls of Blossom Wood

✿ To the Rescue ✿

Catherine Coe

SCHOLASTIC INC.

Echo Mountains
Rushing River
Badger Falls
Moon Chestnut
Oval of Oaks
The Great Hedge

For Cora Cochrane,
with lots of love xxx

Chapter 1
Back to Blossom Wood

"I SO want to go to Blossom Wood again." Eva's green eyes sparkled as she turned to her two best friends, Alex and Katie. They were on their way home from the convenience store after picking up newspapers for their parents.

"So do I," Alex said in her soft voice. She was the smallest and quietest of the

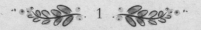

three friends. "But Bobby hasn't left the feather for us. Without it, we can't go back."

A week earlier, Katie, Alex, and Eva had had an amazing adventure when they'd found a white feather inside a hollow tree trunk in Katie's backyard. To their shock, the trunk had started spinning while they were inside. When it slowed down again, their toes had tingled and their fingers had fizzed, and they'd opened their eyes to see that they'd turned into owls! Not only that, they were no longer in Katie's yard—instead, they were high up on a tree branch in the beautiful Blossom Wood. There, they'd met Bobby the badger and many other woodland creatures—and they'd helped save the magical Moon Chestnut tree.

Katie shook her head, and her long

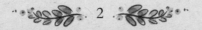

blonde hair swished around her shoulders. "I've checked the tree *every* day! Before school, *and* after! And this morning. But there's been no sign of the feather."

Eva stopped suddenly on the sidewalk. "Why don't we try going back anyway? I really, REALLY want to be an owl again." She looked up at the sky, raised her arms above her bobbed brown hair and imagined flying across the treetops, the wind in her feathers . . .

Katie spun in a circle, her hopes rising. "Do you think that would work?"

Alex grabbed the arms of her two friends. "No—we can't! Bobby promised he would leave the feather there when he needed us. We can't go without it."

"I guess you're right," said Katie, casting her gaze down. The girls began walking again.

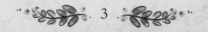

"But we could check again now, just in case," Eva said as they reached Katie's ivy-covered house. She held up a newspaper. "I'll drop this off and then let's meet in your yard, Katie." She ran off to her thatched cottage next door, while Alex skipped to her house—a red-brick bungalow on the other side of Katie's.

"I'll do the same thing." Alex's curly black hair bounced in her bun as she ran. "See you in five minutes!"

Less than two minutes later—since the girls were too excited to wait—Alex and Eva ran into Katie's backyard. They saw Katie at the end of the yard, poking her head out of the hollow trunk of the fallen chestnut tree. Even from a distance they could see her giant smile.

They sprinted over to her.

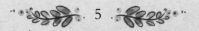

"Is it there? It is, isn't it?" Eva cried, puffing as she slowed to a stop.

Katie grinned, brought out the large, glossy white feather from behind her back, and winked. "How did you know?"

"We could see you smiling from across the yard!" Alex ducked her head into the

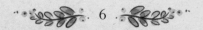

hollow trunk, feeling both excited and nervous about what adventure might be waiting for them in Blossom Wood today.

"Wait." Eva's smile fell from her face. "I'm supposed to be going to an art exhibit with my Mom this morning."

Katie put her hands to her head. "And I have a test at dance class later! Oh, it's not fair!"

But Alex was grinning. "Don't you remember? When we're in Blossom Wood, no time passes back here!"

Katie did a little jump as the knot of disappointment in her stomach was replaced by a ripple of excitement. "Of course!" She ran to the end of the trunk. "Come on—let's go!"

The three girls dived into the large tree trunk one after the other. Just as she'd

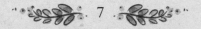

been the first time, Eva was amazed that it seemed bigger on the inside than the outside. Even Katie, the tallest of the three friends, could sit inside easily without her head touching the top.

Once they were all in the trunk, blinking their eyes to adjust to the gloom, Katie held out the feather. "Ready?" she asked her friends, feeling her legs shaking in anticipation.

"Ready!" Eva and Alex replied. They all grabbed one another's hands and closed their eyes tightly.

The spinning started right away— slowly at first, then faster and faster. They squeezed one another's hands harder, and Alex tried not to feel afraid as they spun around and around, wind rushing past her ears. She knew this would take them to Blossom Wood,

after all. It was just that she didn't like carnival rides very much, and this felt just like one!

Katie, on the other hand, couldn't help but let out a long, excited squeal. She loved the feeling of spinning around wildly. "My fingers are tingling! And my toes! We must be almost there!"

She was right: The whistling wind died down and the spinning grew slower— though the girls didn't dare look until they stopped completely.

When it did, Eva opened one eye just a crack. "I can't believe it. We're really back," she breathed. She blinked once, twice, three times at the amazing sight in front of her. They'd arrived on a branch at the top of the Moon Chestnut tree, just as they had before, but today it looked completely different from their first visit. Last time, the tree had been dying, with withered brown leaves and drooping branches. Today, its leaves were huge and green and shiny, and the strong branches stretched up high. Its trunk, a crescent-moon shape which gave the tree its name, looked thick and healthy, and yellow sparkles of sunshine glittered like magic all around it. The beautiful woodland spread out as far as Eva could see—full of towering trees, a sparkling lake, a glistening river, pretty hedges, and shimmering grassland. Animals ran around everywhere, and birds flew on the gentle breeze.

"Look at the tree! We really did save it." Alex loved wildlife and nature, and she'd been wondering how the Moon Chestnut was doing ever since they'd left Blossom Wood. But she didn't need to worry—the tree was healthy and buzzing with life, swarming with the happy birds, squirrels, and insects who lived there.

Alex turned to Katie and gasped. In her excitement to be back, she'd almost forgotten that they were now *owls*! Katie was a beautiful snowy owl, with huge wings and glossy white feathers.

Katie hopped around on the branch. "Wow! It feels even more magical than I remember!" She spread out her wings and leapt off the branch, swooping down to the ground.

Alex looked down at her own body— she was a little owl, the smallest of the three. She shook out her brown wings and swiveled her fluffy head around.

Next to her, Eva was smiling. She was a barn owl with a white body and light-brown wings, and was twice the size of Alex, though still not as big as Katie! "Look at us—we really are owls again!" Eva hooted.

Alex grinned and wondered if they'd ever get used to being such incredible creatures. She fluttered off the branch, feeling a bit more confident about flying this time. She zoomed towards the ground steadily, swooping left and right to avoid the branches in her way.

Eva clapped her wings. "Great flying, Alex!" She jumped from the branch herself, shouting, "Wheeeeeeeeee!" and waving to the animals she recognized as she flew. There was Loulou the squirrel, racing up the tree trunk with a chestnut in her paws; Wilf the caterpillar, shuffling along with a big green chestnut leaf on his back; and Bella the bee, buzzing toward her nest with a mouthful of pollen.

The three friends landed at the base of the tree, giggling.

Then Alex bobbed her little head. "I wonder why Bobby called us here. Nothing seems to be wrong!"

"You're right," said Eva, a smile lighting up her heart-shaped face as she took in the busy woodland. "Everyone seems to be happy!" Along with watching animals going about their daily business, she could hear a twittering tune coming from a thrush, and the songs of sparrows flying high in the sky.

"Maybe we're here just to have fun!" Katie beamed, flapping her wings at the thought. "Ooh, let's go to Willow Lake! I REALLY want to float around on the lily pads there..."

Alex was about to reply when she felt a tap on her shoulder. She swung around and saw a little brown wren hopping from foot to foot. "Hello," said Alex gently. "Is everything OK?"

The pretty bird opened her beak to speak. But, although she kept opening and closing it, nothing came out—not even a squeak!

Chapter 2

Speechless

"Oh, Winnie," Alex said. "What happened?" She remembered Winnie from their first visit to Blossom Wood. In fact, she'd thought back then that Winnie had a very loud voice for such a small bird. But now Winnie seemed to have lost her voice completely!

Winnie looked upward and then fluttered off the ground.

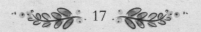

"I think she wants us to follow her," Eva said.

The three friends zoomed up into the sky behind Winnie, wondering where they were headed.

The wren slowed down near the middle of the Moon Chestnut tree and came to rest on a thick branch. As Katie landed next to her, she saw what Winnie was bringing them to—her family's home. It was a beautifully woven nest, made of glossy chestnut leaves and thick green moss. A giant lily-pad umbrella above the nest protected it from rain, and little daisy flower baskets hung from the nest's edges. Six young, sad-looking wrens poked their heads out the moment Winnie arrived—but when they opened their beaks, they didn't make a single sound!

Alex's heart thumped with concern as she hopped along the branch. When she drew closer to the nest she noticed that a couple of Winnie's children had tears glistening in their eyes. The poor birds!

Frowning, Eva turned to Alex and Katie and whispered, "What are we going to do?"

Katie bent down close to the nest. "Do

you know what happened? How did you lose your voices?"

The wrens looked at one another and shrugged. It seemed they had no idea.

"Wait—I can hear something." Alex put her wing to her ear. It was a familiar gravelly voice, coming from the ground.

"Bobby!" Katie smiled, hoping he'd have some answers.

Alex turned to Winnie and her family. "I promise we'll do everything we can to help you," she said solemnly.

"We'll be back soon," Eva added, before giving them a wave and leaping from the branch.

The friendly badger raised a paw in greeting as Alex, Katie, and Eva landed with a rustle on the leaf-covered ground. "Thank treetops, dear owls, for coming so quickly! I see you've already discovered our problem. The poor wrens—they are all very distraught at losing their voices. And it's just SUCH terrible timing!"

Katie tipped her snowy-white head to one side, confused. "What do you mean?"

"The annual Blossom Wood birdsong concert is tomorrow," Bobby explained. "Absolutely *everyone* in the forest will be there—and many creatures from outside Blossom Wood, too. You see, the wrens

always open the concert with a dawn chorus . . . but at the moment, they can't sing a note!"

That's why I can hear so many other birds tweeting in the woods, Eva realized. They were all practicing for the concert! No wonder the wrens were so upset. "Oh, dear," she said, feeling awful for their bird friends.

"Can someone else help out?" Alex had spotted a group of finches singing nearby, with one at the front waving his wings to conduct the rest. "Could some other birds do the dawn chorus instead?"

Bobby shook his stripy head. "Everyone else will be busy performing their own parts in the concert—and besides, the wrens are very proud of the tradition. It's been this way ever since I've lived here—and that's more years than I'd like to admit! They haven't told anyone else, you see, just me, because they don't want to let everyone down. What's a concert without a dawn chorus, after all?"

The three best friends bowed their feathery heads, thinking hard. Just like before, the whole forest was relying on them!

Katie was the first to open her beak. "We could do it!" Her orange eyes lit up as the idea formed in her head. "We could stand in for the wrens!" *It can't be that hard*, she thought. Katie loved singing, and she was in the school choir.

Alex's talons trembled at the suggestion. She didn't like being in the spotlight. But she realized that they had no other choice. As Eva nodded her head in agreement, Alex bobbed hers up and down, too. It was the only way.

Bobby clapped his leathery black paws together. "Owls, I think that's a marvelous idea! I knew you'd be able to help!"

Katie grinned. "We'd better start learning the dawn chorus, if the concert's tomorrow," she said. "How does it go?"

Bobby chuckled. "Oh, you'd better not ask me—I can't sing for chestnuts! But Charles will be able to help you." When the three friends frowned, Bobby explained, "Charles is a blackbird, and he's the Blossom Wood music teacher—he's helped all the birds here sing at one time or another."

Alex felt a little relieved to hear that. "Should we find him right away?"

"Yes, I think you should. He lives in

Apple Orchard. Listen for music as you fly there—you'll be sure to find him then. I should warn you, though: he can sometimes be a *teensy* bit grouchy. But his twit is worse that his tweet, if you know what I mean."

The friends didn't, not really, but they decided it was better not to ask.

"I hope he's not too scary," tweeted Alex as the owls fluttered off the ground, waving goodbye to the friendly old badger.

"Don't worry, Alex," replied Katie, soaring high into the crisp blue sky. "I'm sure he'll be fine. I mean, how bad can a blackbird be?"

Chapter 3
The Wise Owls

Flying over Blossom Wood was just as magical as Alex, Katie, and Eva remembered. They swooped high above the treetops, the wind ruffling their wings. The huge woodland stretched out below them as far as they could see—there was so much to explore here.

Although the sun was shining, the air was cold, and Alex felt glad to have

such fluffy feathers. She guessed it must be wintertime here, because there was a lot more snow on the mountains in the distance than on their first visit to the wood. She flapped her small wings quickly to keep herself warm, and giggled as she watched Katie swoop up high, then zoom down low, as if she were a yo-yo.

"Flying is SO MUCH FUN!" Katie hooted as they crossed Pine Forest and reached Apple Orchard.

Despite the cold, the trees were still laden with apples of every color and size—pale pink, rosy red, emerald green. Alex blinked in surprise. The apple tree in her yard at home never had any fruit in the winter. *Are these trees magical?* she wondered.

"What's that noise?" Eva slowed down,

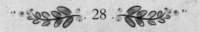

floating in mid-air for a moment. "Can you hear music?"

Katie stopped with a loop-the-loop and listened to the drumming sound wafting up from below. "Yes! Is it Charles?"

"I think it might be," said Alex, her little voice barely audible. She suddenly felt nervous again.

"There's only one way to find out!" Eva tipped her head forward and began hurtling to the ground. Alex winced as her rather clumsy friend clipped the leaves of a Golden Delicious tree and went spinning downwards. Fortunately, the soft mossy ground acted as a cushion and Eva bounced as she landed headfirst.

"Whoops!" Eva lay on the ground for a moment. Alex and Katie landed next to her much more carefully, laughing when they saw she wasn't hurt. They held out

their wings to pull her up. They were used to Eva falling over a lot—she was always covered in bruises and bumps.

"Well," came a deep, snooty voice. "I hope you have a very good reason to be interrupting this drum lesson."

The three best friends jumped and turned around.

At the foot of a Granny Smith tree stood a large, glossy blackbird, his tail fanned out, his wings on his hips. In front of him, five bright-green frogs sat behind pinecone drums. Even though the blackbird was smaller than Alex, she felt a little frightened. She tried to remember what Bobby had said. Something about the blackbird's tweet— or was it his twit?

Luckily, Katie took charge. "Hi, Charles! Bobby sent us to ask if you could give us some singing lessons. Would that be OK?"

The bird raised his eyebrows. "It's *Mr. Blackbird* to you! Well, you can't have a lesson now—surely you can see I'm busy. You'll have to come back later— this afternoon. But I'll need to be paid, you know . . . some thick, bendy twigs will do nicely, to warm up my nest now that winter's here. Do you think you can manage that?" He peered at them closely.

Eva, Katie, and Alex nodded, not daring to open their beaks.

Charles waved a wing dismissively. "Be off with you, then—I'll see you at two o'clock sharp!"

The three friends didn't need to be told twice, not where grumpy blackbirds were concerned. As the frogs began tapping the pine cones with their little webbed hands, the owls flew off above the trees of Apple Orchard.

They'd just started collecting twigs in nearby Pine Forest when Katie heard a tiny voice below her: "Oh, excuse me! Can you help me?"

Katie looked down. A bright-red

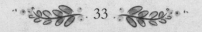

ladybug was jumping up and down. At least she *thought* it was a ladybug, though it didn't have any spots. Katie picked the creature up gently in her wing. "What's the matter, little thing?"

The ladybug's eyes turned down sadly. "I've lost my spots! Oh, where are they?

Can you wise owls help me find them?"

Katie opened her beak to reply but—just like the wrens—she was speechless. She'd never seen a ladybug without spots, and she had no idea where they might be!

Eva came to her rescue. "Can you remember when you last had them?"

"Oh, urm . . . no . . . I can't remember! But they must be somewhere!" The ladybug bounced around Katie's wing.

Alex flew close to the creature. "Ladybug," she began gently, remembering something she'd once read in a library book, "Maybe you didn't lose them, but you just never had spots in the first place. That makes you extra special, you know—there aren't many ladybugs with no spots at all."

"Do you think? Oh, that is exciting! It's

nice to be special. Thank you, owls!" With that, the funny little ladybug fluttered her tiny wings and shot away into the dense pine trees.

The friends went back to searching for twigs, hopping over the ground and carefully picking up sticks in their talons. As Alex plucked up a particularly long pine twig, a red fox with a white-tipped tail dashed over to them.

"Hey, owls, you've gotta help me!" He scratched at both ears furiously with his back paws. "These fleas—I can't get rid of them. I just wanna be clean! Can you help?"

The owls glanced at each other, not sure what to say. Katie wished they were as wise as everybody in Blossom Wood seemed to think!

Then Eva had an idea. When her cat got fleas, her mom always gave him an

herbal bath. "Try rosemary leaves," she suggested. "Pick a handful, and stir them into your bath water. That should help."

"Oh, owls, thank you! You really are as smart as they say!" With one last scratch, the fox scampered off through a thick patch of ferns.

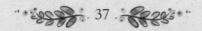

"That poor fox—his fleas looked pretty bad." Eva rubbed her tummy with a talon. Seeing the fox like that made her feel itchy, too. "Oh! What's that?" Something wet and slimy had bounced into her tail feathers. She looked down and saw a red-speckled toad staring back up at her.

"Ribbit! I'm so sorry," the toad croaked. "Ribbit! You see, I'm lost! Ribbit! Can't find my pond! I mean lake. Ribbit! Yes, I think that's where I live!"

"Do you mean Willow Lake—the one with all the lily pads?" Alex asked.

"Ribbit! That's the one!"

"Then you're a long way from home." Katie felt sorry for the confused creature. "Hop on my wing, and I'll fly you back there."

"Oh, ribbity ribbit. That would be wonderful!" The toad jumped on and grabbed hold of Katie's feathers. With a flap of her wings, they were soon flying up into the clear blue sky.

"I'll be back soon!" Katie called over her shoulder.

Eva watched them leave. "Well, at least

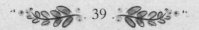

we're helping some of the animals here . . .
I just wish we knew the answer to how
to get the wrens' voices back!"

Alex bobbed her head. "I know . . .
but, anyway, we'd better get faster
at collecting twigs. Otherwise we'll
never have enough in time for our
singing lesson!"

Chapter 4

A Special Sleepover

That afternoon, with their twigs gripped in their talons, Katie, Eva, and Alex zoomed back towards Apple Orchard. This time, Eva was careful to fly down slowly, and the three friends all landed gracefully in front of Charles.

The blackbird didn't even seem to notice their arrival—he was bent over a leaf scrawled with writing, tapping his bright-orange beak across it as he read.

Katie coughed. "Ahem. Mr. Blackbird?"

Charles swung his head towards them, his beak set in a scowl. But when he glanced down and saw the masses of twigs in their talons, his black eyes twinkled. "I see you've brought payment. That looks like just enough!"

Alex breathed out slowly in relief. "Will you be able to teach us the dawn chorus?"

Charles raised his fluffy eyebrows. "That's the most difficult song of all—in fact, only the wrens have mastered it! I highly recommend that you start with something simpler."

The owls' faces fell.

"*Please*, Mr. Blackbird, can we try the dawn chorus?" Eva pleaded. "It's for the concert tomorrow—the wrens have lost their voices and we need to stand in for them!"

"Oh, dear me." Charles sighed deeply. "OK, then—let's give it a try. But let me hear your singing voices first and see what we've got to work with." He pointed a wing at Katie. "Snowy owl, you first!"

Katie stepped forward confidently, remembering everything she'd learned about singing. She took a deep breath, filling her chest, and out came . . . a horrible barking-squeal noise! She clapped a wing over her beak, horrified, and turned to her two friends. "But I sing really well at school, don't I?"

"Maybe you're just out of practice," said Alex, nudging Katie with a wing before she said too much. The animals in the wood didn't know that the owls were really girls. When they first met Bobby, they'd tried to explain it to him, but the badger hadn't understood at all. Alex didn't think Charles would believe them either.

The blackbird rolled his eyes and shook his head as if he'd heard such excuses many times before. He nodded at Eva. "Barn owl, let's hear you next."

The only place Eva ever sang was in the shower. Still, she couldn't let the wrens down. She closed her eyes, imagining she was back at home, in her bathroom. She opened her beak slowly . . . and closed it again quickly when a high-pitched screech came out!

Eva opened her eyes and saw that Charles had put his wings over his ears. He lowered them slowly now that Eva

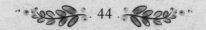

had stopped screeching. "Oh, dear, oh, dear. Come on, owls, you have to do better than that!" The blackbird turned his beady gaze to Alex. "Little owl, your turn now."

Alex stood on one leg, her little head bobbing up and down nervously. She was sure she wouldn't be any better than her friends. She never sang at all—she was much too shy. She tried to think of an excuse to get out of it, but then remembered the sad-looking wrens. Alex realized she had to try, for their sakes. She breathed in and out a few times, puffed up her chest and . . . a little low hooting noise whistled out. It didn't sound that bad to Alex—but what would the blackbird think?

"*Better* . . . though that's not saying much, considering the first two attempts!"

Charles glared at Katie and Eva. "Now I'll sing the dawn-chorus tune, and you repeat after me . . ."

The three friends did their best to follow the tune, but with their new owl singing voices it was very, very tricky. Katie's voice kept coming out as a bark-squeal, and Eva's was super-screechy, no matter how deeply she breathed. Alex managed a fairly tuneful hoot, but together they sounded more like a group of wailing cats than a pretty chorus of birds. But they kept on trying—again and again and again.

Despite his grumpiness, Charles was very patient. Alex started to realize that he was, in fact, a very good teacher.

"It's getting dark, owls," the blackbird suddenly announced. "We'll have to stop now. You'd better come back at first

light—we need all the time we have left to prepare for the concert!"

Surprised, Katie looked up. Sure enough, the sun had set, turning the sky an indigo blue with stars twinkling like tiny fireworks. They'd been practicing for hours!

"We'd better go home," said Alex, her head bobbing. "It's getting late!"

"But we can't leave yet," twittered Katie. "We've got to be here for the concert tomorrow! Right, Eva?"

Eva's green eyes grew serious. "Yes, we have to stay." She put a wing around Alex and gave her a squeeze. "Remember what you said—while we're here, no time will pass at home, so we won't be missed. And we'll get to have a magical Blossom Wood sleepover!"

That made Alex feel better. "You're right. But can we check on the wrens before we go to bed? We haven't seen them all day."

Katie smiled at her caring friend. "Of course!"

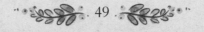

Charles was already arranging
the twigs into piles for his nest,
whistling a jazzy tune as he worked.
They thanked him for the singing lesson
and promised they'd return first thing
the next morning, then flew back to
the Moon Chestnut tree. Although their

owl eyesight meant they could see in the dark easily, they didn't especially need to tonight—their journey was lit by the full moon that rose over Blossom Wood, making the woodland sparkle and shine in its beautiful glare.

Alex was the first to land on the wrens' branch of the Moon Chestnut tree. She hopped over to the cute nest quickly when she saw that Winnie was shivering. "You're cold!" The wrens' feathers looked much thinner than the owls'—they didn't seem to keep the little birds warm the way Alex's did, not in this wintry weather.

Of course, the wren couldn't reply, but Alex had an idea. She waited for Eva to land beside her, then whispered in her ear.

Eva smiled, nodded, and leaped off the branch again.

"What's she doing?" asked Katie,

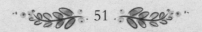

making the branch wobble as she landed next to Alex.

"Wait and see!" Alex gave her friend a wink.

Minutes later, Eva swooped back to the tree, holding something green in her little beak. She dropped it into the wrens' nest.

"A scarf?" Katie peered at the fluffy thing made of moss and grasses. Eva loved art and crafts, and was always giving her friends presents that she'd made.

"Winnie looked so cold," Alex explained, then turned to the wren. "We hope it will keep you warmer tonight."

Winnie gave her a small smile and mouthed, "Thank you!"

They wanted to make sure *all* the wrens were warm, so Katie and Alex collected moss and grass while Eva sat beside their nest, knitting scarves. She used two long, thin twigs, which tapped together as she worked in the light of the moon. Soon, each of the seven wrens had a pretty scarf wrapped around his or her neck. They huddled together, smiling, their eyes droopy with tiredness.

Eva yawned. "Goodnight, wrens. We should be getting to sleep, too!"

"Really?" Katie made a face. She always had lots of energy, and hated going to bed. But she knew tomorrow would be a busy day, and she noticed that her friends looked as tired as the wrens did. "Oh . . . OK. But *where* will we sleep?"

"What's up, owls?" a squeaky voice interrupted them.

Alex looked over to see Loulou the squirrel scampering down the Moon Chestnut trunk. She came to a skidding stop alongside the owls.

"We need somewhere to sleep tonight," Eva tweeted. "Can you help?"

With a swish of her tail, Loulou grinned. "Of course—there's plenty of room in Blossom Wood! In fact, I know just the tree, over in the Oval of Oaks. Follow me!" Without taking a breath, she darted away.

The owls waved goodnight to the wrens and flew above the excited squirrel. They watched as she shot up one of the tallest oak trees nearby.

"This one will be perfect for you!" Loulou called.

The three friends swooped in to land on a branch and immediately saw what Loulou meant. There was a large hollow near the bottom of the trunk, perfect for Katie; a medium-sized hole in the middle, just right for Eva; and a small one at the top, an exact fit for Alex!

"Thank you so much!" hooted Alex as she jumped into her little hollow filled with soft leaves and grasses that looked even cozier than a blanket. She flapped around, feeling both worried and excited. She wasn't used to sleeping away from home—but she also couldn't wait to have a sleepover in a magical forest!

"Hello!" said a tiny, high-pitched voice. Alex turned to see two gray mice. "I'm Mo and this is May." Mo's nose twitched rapidly as he spoke. "We live in this tree, too. Loulou told us you're staying here tonight. We wanted to make you feel at home, so we've brought you a cup of hot nettle milk. It'll help you sleep!"

May nodded. "And if you need anything else, you can find us through the little doorway right at the bottom of the trunk."

Alex took the acorn cup in a wing and smiled at the kind, generous mice. "Thank you!" she called as they scurried down the trunk to deliver cups of milk to Katie and Eva, too. Alex drank the delicious, creamy milk in one gulp, and felt her eyelids grow heavy. "Goodnight," she yawned.

"Sleep tight," hooted Eva.

"See you in the morning light!" Katie finished the rhyme they always sang at sleepovers.

Before they knew it, each of the best friends had drifted off to sleep to the magical sounds of night-time hoots, rustles, and whistles in the wonderful Blossom Wood.

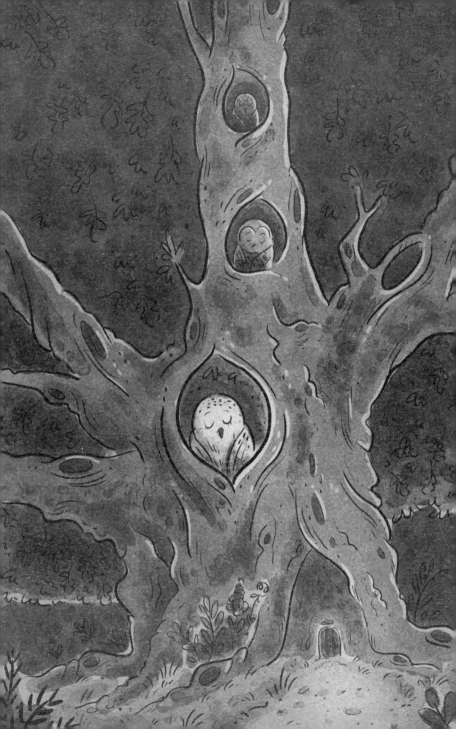

Chapter 5
Feeling the Cold

Eva opened her eyes. For a moment, she had no idea where she was . . . Why could she see thick green trees all around her, and the ground far below, glistening with dew? Then her beak fell open as she remembered: she, Katie, and Alex were in Blossom Wood, and they were no longer girls—they were owls!

She stretched her wings, then fluttered out of her soft, warm hollow in the tall oak tree. She hopped around on a branch feeling refreshed and awake—though it had been strange to be an owl and sleep standing up!

"Good morning!" she cried, flying up to the entrance of Alex's hollow, just above hers. "Can you believe it? Our first ever sleepover in Blossom Wood!"

Alex bobbed her little head. "I know— it's awesome!"

The two friends fluttered down to find Katie, but when they ducked their feathery heads into her hollow, Katie's eyes were closed.

"Katie," Alex called gently.

Nothing but gentle snores came from Katie's beak.

Eva gave her a little poke.

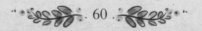

"Ahhh, w-w-what!" Startled, Katie opened her eyes wide and flapped her wings, jumping around in circles. "Where am I?" She looked down at her snowy-white body. "And *what* am I?!"

Alex put a wing on Katie's. "It's OK— we're in Blossom Wood, remember?"

Katie's orange eyes grew huge, then she let out a big belly laugh. "Of course! Wow—I'd forgotten for a minute!" The three friends giggled together, feeling excited to be there all over again.

Alex pointed a wing at the pearly-pink sky. "We should get over to Pine Forest to see Charles. He told us to come at first light, remember?" The Blossom Wood birdsong concert was later that morning. Alex trembled, trying not to think about having to perform the dawn chorus in front of everyone. It was too scary for words.

Eva nodded. "We have a lot of practicing to do!"

"And Charles is bound to be super-grouchy if we're late!" Katie hopped out of her hollow and on to a branch, then leapt off it into the chilly early-morning air. "Brrrr, it's colder than ever today!" she said, flapping her large wings quickly to keep warm.

As soon as the three friends soared into the dawn sky, they heard a voice behind them. It was the last voice they were expecting to hear.

"Owls, wait!"

Eva spun around. It was Winnie! Eva was so shocked to hear her voice that she forgot to keep flapping her wings, and fell like a stone for a moment before quickly fluttering them again.

"Winnie!" Katie zoomed towards the tiny bird. "You can speak!" She dipped her head and spun a loop-the-loop in happiness.

Alex flew closer to Winnie, opening her yellow beak wide in a huge smile. "When did your voice come back?"

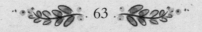

In her excitement, Winnie flapped her
wings even faster than usual, and she
bobbed about in the air. "I woke up
this morning, yawned . . . and a loud
twittering-tweet came right out! I was
so diddly-do happy that I began singing,
which woke up my children—and they
can all speak, too!"

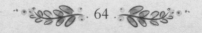

The owls spun around in delight. "That's fantastic!" yelled Katie. "But I wonder—what happened?"

Alex noticed the mossy, green scarf Winnie had wrapped around her neck. "It must be the scarves!"

Winnie frowned. "What do you mean?"

"I think being so cold made you lose your voices. When you warmed up, they came back again!"

The pretty wren somersaulted in the air. "Of course!"

Katie was already racing off toward the Moon Chestnut tree, calling over her feathery shoulder, "Come on—let's go and celebrate with the rest of the wrens!"

As they neared the special tree, they heard the final preparations for the concert going on all around. A robin choir stood in a circle tweeting beautiful harmonies, while sparrows lined up on a low branch of the Moon Chestnut, trilling and whistling. Above, goldfinches flew between the trees, calling out a song in perfect tune. *If this is a taste of the concert,* Eva thought, *it's going to be amazing!*

Winnie led the way to her lovely nest. "Let the win-diddly-wonderful owls hear your voices!" she told her children. The wrens looked at one another, opened their mouths slowly, and . . . out came a tweet, a twit, and a whistle! Then a trill and a squill, a twitter and a tweep! Soon the nest was jumping with excited young wrens all singing together.

Katie, Alex, and Eva clapped their wings as the wrens sang, feeling both delighted and mightily relieved.

"I'm so glad you all have your voices back!" twittered Alex, a warm wave of

happiness flooding her body.

Eva grinned, stretching her heart-shaped face wide. "Me too. Not just because you can sing—but because we don't have to!"

"What do you mean?" asked Winnie, a frown of confusion clouding her face.

"We had singing lessons with Charles," Katie explained. "We thought we could stand in for you at the concert if your voices didn't come back in time."

"Oh, that's so splendiferously lovely of you. To put in all that effort!" Winnie opened her little wings out wide. "But you'll still sing with us, won't you?"

Eva, Alex, and Katie gulped. *Uh-oh!* How could they say no?

Chapter 6
The Best Birdsong Ever

Foxglove Glade was even busier than
the first time the owls had been here,
when they'd had a meeting about saving
the Moon Chestnut tree. Hundreds—
maybe even thousands—of birds, animals,
and insects filled the colorful arena.
The circular, grassy glade was lined with
beautiful, delicate foxgloves in every

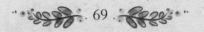

color imaginable, so bright they seemed to glow, making the whole area look magical. At one side of the glade, a stage sloped upward, backed by light-pink foxgloves. Katie recognized many of the creatures here, including Ruby the rabbit and her son Billy, Bella the bee, and Loulou the squirrel. She saw the red fox they'd helped the day before, who was no longer scratching but beaming instead, and there was the ladybug with no spots, too! The crisp winter air buzzed with chattering animals, and Katie's talons were tingling—she felt very, very special just to be there.

"It's the biggest audience we've ever had for the birdsong concert!" Bobby whispered as they stood behind a tree next to the stage.

Alex's wings shook. She, Eva, and Katie

had agreed to sing with the wrens—they just couldn't say no after they'd been asked so nicely—but they'd had no more time to practice with Charles, and Alex knew their voices were worse than terrible.

At that moment the sun broke through a fluffy white cloud, shining down into the glade. It made the foxgloves around the edge light up like stage lights. Not for the first time, Alex decided Blossom Wood was the most magical place she'd ever seen. This thought calmed her nerves and she reached out to hold the wingtips of her two best friends.

Katie winked at her. "We can do this," she said.

Eva grinned. "But it's probably best if we don't sing too loudly . . ."

Alex bobbed her head. She'd already been planning on that!

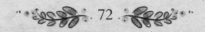

"Good luck, dearest owls," Bobby said to them before striding out onto the stage. He'd swapped his usual scarf for a cute little bow tie.

The glade erupted in applause and Alex gripped the wings of her friends more tightly. She felt as if her heart might leap out of her fluffy chest.

Bobby padded to the center of the stage, stood up on his hind paws, and

began addressing the audience. "Thank you all so very much for attending our annual birdsong concert here in the *wonderful* Blossom Wood—even if I do say so myself! I know that many of you have come from faraway forests and fields, and for that we are truly grateful. We have a magnificent lineup of birdsong for you this year, including three extra-special guests! So without further ado, please put your paws, pads, hooves, and wings together for the dawn chorus, performed by the wren family—plus Eva, Katie, and Alex, the owls of Blossom Wood!"

The clapping came again, even louder now, as the wrens fluttered to the stage. Katie, Alex, and Eva hopped out and stood in a row behind them. Winnie, in the middle of the line of wrens, looked around. "Good luck!" she whispered to the owls. "You'll be fan–doobly-tastic!"

Katie smiled back, though her nerves were janglier than they'd been at her first ballet recital. But there was no more time to wait, because Winnie was counting them in with the wave of a wing . . . and the song began.

The wrens' dawn chorus was beautiful, with lots of harmonies, rising lilts, and crescendos. Luckily, it was also extremely loud, and Eva relaxed as it became clear that no one could hear their screechy-barky owl voices over the wrens' delightful tones. From the bees to the bullfrogs, the foxes to the fawns, the audience swayed from side to side with giant smiles on their faces. Everyone seemed to love it!

As Winnie brought a wing up to signal the last few notes of the song, Alex realized she was enjoying herself, and felt a little sad that it was about to end. She'd never performed on a stage before, and there was something truly magical about

making an audience so happy.

The crowd clapped and hooted and yelled their congratulations. Eva felt her face burn with pride—she was pleased to be a part of the dawn chorus, even if no one had really heard her screechy singing.

Next, the robins performed their "Winter Harmony," with lots of bells and rings. Eva thought it sounded just like Christmas. Then the sparrows sang a fast-paced song called "Whistle in the Wood," and the goldfinches put on a spectacular display high over the glade, performing their "Soaring High" tune while they flew.

Finally, a group of young starlings, conducted by Charles, finished the concert with a bouncy melody called "Blossom Wood Bop," accompanied by the frog pinecone drum band. As this last piece came to an end, the audience roared. The rabbits stomped their feet, the bees buzzed their wings, the mice clapped their paws, and the deer tapped their hooves. The noise grew as loud as thunder as Bobby shuffled to the stage once more and beckoned all the birds to join him.

They all squeezed onto the slope, their wings around one another. At the back, Eva, Katie, and Alex clasped each other's wingtips. They kept grinning, though their beaks ached from smiling so much!

"I must declare this the best birdsong concert EVER!" Bobby croaked deeply. "And I've seen a lot of them in my time! The birds were simply fabulous,

their songs stunning, and you've been an amazing audience."

Everyone applauded again, and the birds gave a fluttery bow.

As the audience began moving away from their seats to leave the glade, the birds started hopping down from the stage.

Winnie flew over to Eva, Alex, and Katie. "Thank you SO much for joining our dawn chorus. It was such an honor to have you sing with us little wrens!"

The three best friends beamed. "It was our pleasure!" hooted Eva, wondering if Winnie was just being polite or whether she simply hadn't heard their voices.

"We were wondering," Winnie continued, "whether you might like to join our choir full-time!"

Alex raised her eyebrows. So Winnie

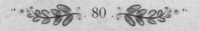

really *had* been serious about their singing! Katie put a snowy-white wing around Winnie. "I'm very sorry, but I'm afraid we can't. It wouldn't be fair, since we're not here all the time. But we'd love to join choir practice when we *are* in the woods—if that's OK with you."

"Oh, yip-diddly-yes!" Winnie spun round, pleased, and flew off to join the rest of her wren family.

"I guess we should be getting back," twittered Eva.

Katie and Alex nodded sadly. They didn't really want to go home, but now they'd solved the wrens' problem, they knew that they should.

A deep, snooty voice stopped them in their tracks. "You, there!"

The three friends turned . . . and their hearts sank to their talons. Charles—or

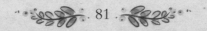

rather, Mr. Blackbird—was hopping toward them. Alex remembered that they'd missed their lesson with him first thing that morning—they'd been on their way there when Winnie had appeared with her voice back. Alex bobbed her head, worrying about how angry he would be.

"Owls, I just wanted to say . . ."

Katie held her breath, waiting to be scolded by the blackbird.

". . . how pleased I am that you solved the wrens' problem! I was absolutely delighted to hear they have their voices back. Good job!"

Eva nearly toppled over from her shock. "Um, thank you," she hooted.

"Now, I must go and congratulate the other birds. But good job again—very well done!" Charles hopped away without another word.

"I'm so glad we're leaving Blossom
Wood with everyone happy—even
Mr. Blackbird!" Katie beamed.

"It's been another amazing adventure!"
said Eva.

Alex reached up and put her two little
wings around her much taller friends.
"And I can't wait for the next one!"

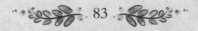

As the Blossom Wood creatures celebrated their best ever birdsong concert, the three friends flew together to the Moon Chestnut tree. They landed in a row on a branch near the top—the one they always arrived on and which would take them back to Katie's yard.

"Ready?" tweeted Katie.

"Ready!" Eva and Alex replied.

They held wingtips, took in the glittering beauty of Blossom Wood for one last time that day, then closed their eyes. The familiar spinning started up, and the wind whooshed past their ears. Soon they'd be back home, girls once again. But they didn't mind—from helping the wrens to joining the concert, they'd had the most amazing time. They just hoped they wouldn't have to wait too long to return!

Did You Know?

❀ Wrens really do have very loud voices for birds so small. The next time you're in the woods or park, see if you can spot—and hear—one.

❀ It's less common, but some ladybugs really don't have any spots!

❀ Owls really do sleep standing up.

❀ Although you might sometimes see foxes rummaging around in trash, they like to be clean—which is why the fox was so upset when he had fleas!

❀ Blackbirds fan out their tails when they're angry—which is what Charles did when the owls interrupted his drum lesson!

Look out for more

The Owls of Blossom Wood

adventures!

Dolphin School

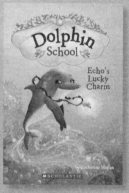

Going to dolphin school
under the sea is magical fun
for Pearl and her friends!